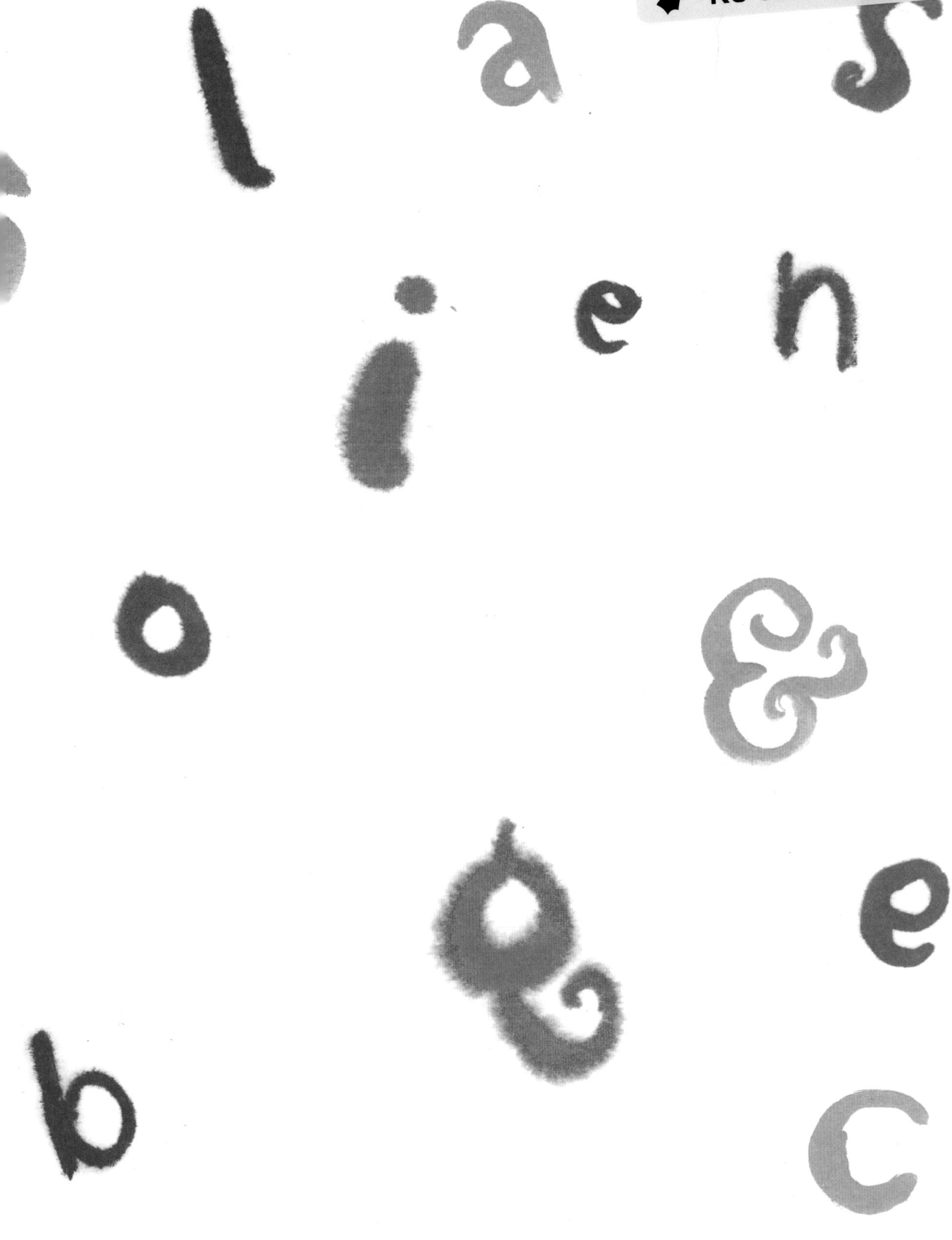

for azia, oscar, india & grace

Published by Pucci Books Ltd on behalf of
Maggie and Rose in 2008

Maggie and Rose Ltd
58 Pembroke Road
Kensington
London W8 6NX

Pucci Books Ltd
32 Great Sutton Street
Clerkenwell
London EC1V 0NB

© Maggie and Rose Ltd 2008

A CIP catalogue record of this book is available
from the British Library.

ISBN 978-0-9559352-3-7

Printed in Portugal

maggie   rose   oscar  & bentley

maggie & rose's
lovely story

by
mr z

These are two very pretty girls called
Maggie and Rose. I am taller than Maggie
but she doesn't mind.

Shhhh!

This is our secret club where we do all sorts of very important and top secret stuff.

This is our friend Oscar. He comes to our
club ALL the time. He thinks he's a superhero
but he's just a stinky boy. The only super
thing he's ever done is once he ate 3 ice
creams in a row. We all shouted 'Oscar you
CAN'T' but he DID and then he was sick ...
.... Ewwww!   This is his dog Bentley,
he's ALWAYS hungry but he's very cute. →

Here we are inside our secret clubhouse (shh hh). We can do EVERYTHING you could think of in here, like cooking

and painting

and making things.

whoops. oscar

On this day my Uncle Fabiola
was coming to visit from America,
so we were preparing
some nice things for him.

He always brings us
EXTRAORDINARY
presents....

....One time he brought us a baby fire-breathing dragon but the Police took him away because he kept setting fire to things.

Then another time he brought us REAL Mexican jumping beans, but we kept banging our heads on the ceiling so our mothers took THEM away.

In honour of
Uncle's visit
maggie baked a
yummy cake
all by herself.

But poor maggie,
the cake collapsed
in the
middle.

oh dea

No Fear!
Rose to the rescue!
And I whipped some cream to fill the hole with.

Oscar did a painting of Bentley, this is all he EVER paints, but Shhhh! don't say anything as he gets very cross.

Rat - a - tat - atta - tat!   We knew it was

Uncle Fabiola, he has such a funny way of knocking.

'Hey Kiddoes! How Y'all doin?'
He has a funny way of talking too
'I've brought you these presents

all the way from New Yoik,

I hopes you like em'

oscar

'Please Uncle'
I had to say while we
were opening them,
'please don't smile,
your teeth are SO white
it hurts our eyes.'

And what was
in the parcels?......

..... Scooters!

'Oh no, sorry Uncle, but we've already got scooters, mine's pink!'

'No fear kiddoes, these aren't boring snoring scooters, these are **MAGIC** scooters.

Press this button, hold on tight and they can fly
through the air. The only thing you MUST remember
is they DON'T work on Sundays,
don't ask me why'
'Is today Sunday?'
asked Maggie.
'No its Saturday'
'HOORAY!'

Oscar and Bentley made a rush for the door
but I said NO! 'me and Maggie have
very nicely made a cake which we have to
eat first ' Oscar pretended not to like it
but he had about 100 slices! Then we went
outside to try our new scooters.

oh crumbs

We were just about to press the
magic buttons when we saw a lovely
old lady with a pink handbag and lots
of little dogs. She looked worried.
'Children' she said 'please
help me if you don't mind,
I have lost one of my lovely dogs,
he went that way'
and she pointed towards
Big Ben.

'No fear' I told her, 'We'll find your dog, we can fly! We'll meet you at Big Ben when we've got him.' 'Flying children' she said, 'Whatever next?'

Finally it was time to press the magic buttons. It was soooo exciting. We zoomed up into the sky like rockets, then wooshed about like birds. Maggie was a bit scared at first, but she is quite small.

We flew all over the rooftops, it was
the best fun in the world.
We waved at the people in
the London Eye,

then we went to Trafalgar
Square where we pulled
funny faces at Lord Nelson
on his column, which was a bit
naughty. Then I noticed that
it had got dark and
we could hardly see.

Also,
we had completely
forgotten to look for
the Old Lady's dog, whoops!
to fly to the moon to
Oscar wanted
really was made of cheese. I had
see if it
to tell him that if he had ANY manners
he'd forget about cheese and come
and apologise to the Old Lady.

Oscar and Bentley made us land our scooters next to a sausage stall because they were starving, and there was the old Lady with ALL her dogs. 1, 2, 3, 4, 5   HOORAY!
  'Hello' she said, 'thank you for looking for my dog all this time. The naughty boy ran all the way to this nice man's sausage stall. Luckily he looked after him and I spotted them on my way to Big Ben. We've been chatting ever since, goodness me it's nearly midnight!'

Just then there was a terrible puff of wind and the pretty headscarf on the Old Lady's head blew right off and got caught on Big Ben's big hand. 'Oh no!' she said, 'my favourite headscarf! It was given to me by Chief Willy Nilly, his wife painted the spots on it herself!'

BONG !

BONG !

NG !

We let Oscar and Bentley go after it.
Then the clock started bonging the
midnight chimes. It was VERY loud
BONG BONG BONG
it went. Me and maggie were
very worried because Uncle Fabiola
had warned us that the Scooters
wouldn't fly on Sundays and when the
bongs finished it would be Sunday.

BONG!

BONG!

'QUICKLY OSCAR!' we shouted,
and Bentley stuck out his paw
and grabbed the headscarf just
as the last BONG! bonged.
Then the scooter lost its magic
and
floated
back
down
to the
ground.

real diamonds

The Old Lady was very pleased to get her headscarf back and then she said we should all go back to the palace for a midnight feast ..PALACE? we all exclaimed. 'Oh yes' she said, didn't you guess it? I'm the QUEEN, come on I'm starving.

And so we all scootered back to the palace for the superest midnight feast EVER. There were cakes and gold and real soldiers. But best of all....

..Uncle Fabiola was there too and he had bought us all sunglasses so he could smile as much as he wanted and none of us would be too dazzled by his nice white teeth.

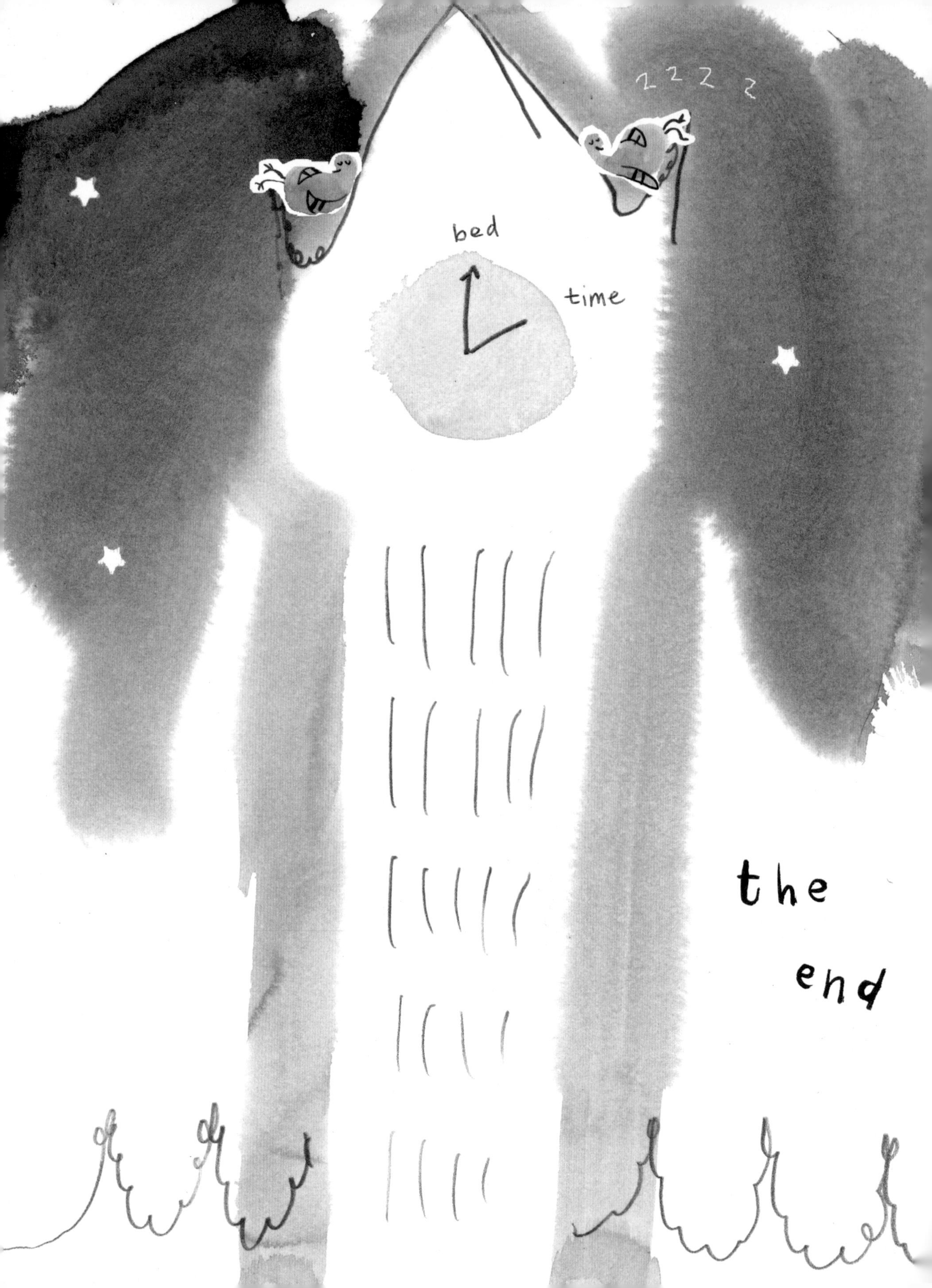

z z z z
bed
time
the
end

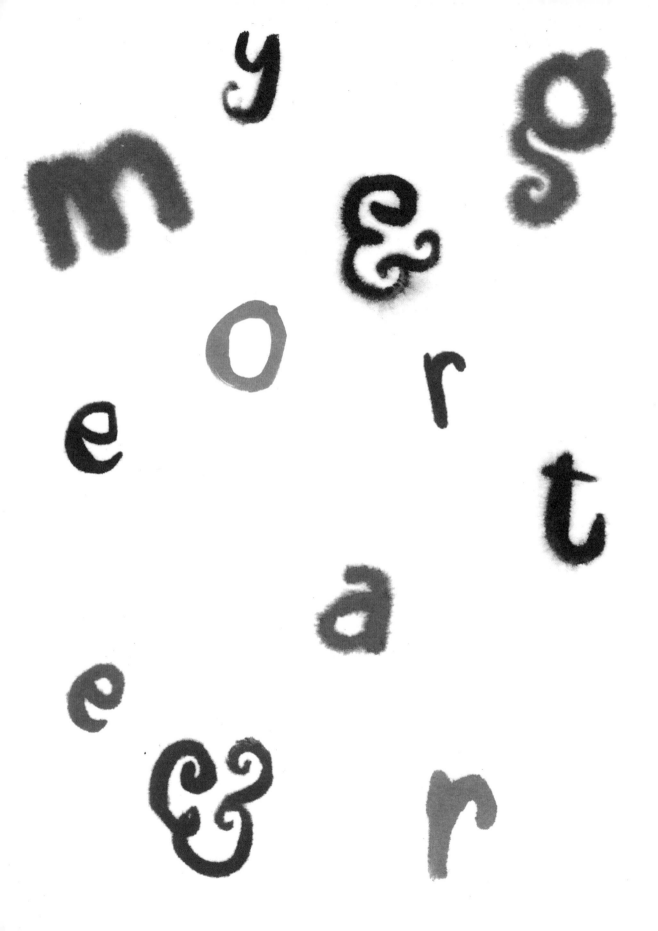